The first of the Tikaboo Tales!

Dedicated to all the creatures who
can't speak up for themselves

ISBN 978-0-9955358-5-5
Printed sustainably by Digital Printing Ireland
Designed in iStudio Publisher

Icicle on his Bicycle

The Misunderstood Husky

Story & Illustrations

by Vivienne Lynch

I know a Husky, Icicle,
a splendid hound you'd like,
who trekked the landscape dashing off,
astride his mountain bike.

Come hail or shine, he'd bike to see
the miles of evergreen.
His forest trails would lead to lands
he'd so far never seen.

No distance was too far for him
- he loved the open space,
the exercise, the Great Outdoors,
the fresh air in his face.

He'd go on great adventures and
make new friends everywhere.
Whenever sad, he's grab his bike
to go and get fresh air.

Because he loved to travel so,
to peddle and explore,
no fence or wall could hold him back,
he'd scarper out the door!

6

Though he was often fostered by
some lovely families,
they found it hard to tolerate
his likelihood to flee.

So Icicle would end up being
passed on from home to home,
but seldom would they keep him as
they knew he loved to roam.

While he explored the forests green
and wandered off the track,
those families would search for him
and call him to come back.

Though Icicle did try his best
to listen and be good,
his lust for life would mean that he
was seldom understood.

While on his latest escapade,
he strayed far from the park
and by the time he made it home,
it was already dark.

Awaiting him, his Foster Mum
declared she'd had enough!
And so he went up to his room
and packed up all his stuff.

With heavy heart and quivering lip,
he mutely took his leave;
for having caused so much distress,
he truly was bereaved.

And so our hero pedalled off
and covered miles that day;
with no specific route in mind,
poor Husky lost his way.

Alone he was on brand new trails,
forlorn and now quite scared.
The shadows soon crept in on him
but this time no-one cared.

16

He sat amidst the pine trees,
feeling lonely, hurt and scared.
Poor Icicle was whining while
a raven overheard.

As Raven contemplated this
poor creature shake with sobs,
he couldn't but feel pity for
the howling, troubled dog.

"That Husky needs some cheering up,
perhaps a kindly word",
and not requiring further thought,
thus spoke our dear old bird:

"Good evening to you, young man,
and welcome to this place ...
I haven't seen you here before,
can't say I know your face."

Our husky dog thought to himself:
"How wonderfully absurd!
How marvellous it is to meet
a real-life talking bird!"

He politely introduced himself
and shyly dried his eyes,
while bravely sniffing back his tears
and trying not to cry:

"It's nice to meet you, Sir", he said
"I think I've lost my way.
I don't know where I'm going though
I've cycled miles today".

The wise bird said: "I'll get my map,
but first let's have some tea.
I'll go and get my glasses then
we'll have some bread and cheese."

20

"Why, thank you", said the grateful dog,
"I've quite an appetite!
Though soon I should be on my way
before it's dark tonight."

"You are most welcome", said the bird,
"Now make yourself at home.
No need is there to roam about,
in darkness all alone.

I see that you're an Arctic breed.
Superb!" wise Raven said.
"So, do you have a sledding team
and do you have a sled?"

"I do not know what "sledding" is
nor friends have I no more.
Indeed my foster mother has
at long last closed the door."

22

"There is no one who loves me now,
I have nowhere to go.
To all of those who know me I'm
a nuisance, don't you know".

With those sad words, our hero wept
as if his heart were broke.
His spirit seemed so hopeless now
with every word he spoke.

The Raven was profoundly moved
by such a wretched sight,
so he and our sad Husky would
talk late into the night.

On pondering his story then
Wise Raven understood
how Icicle had ended up
forlorn within the woods.

Raven said:

"Now just because you're spirited
and cycle everywhere,
that does not mean you're mischievous
- you simply need fresh air!

It's natural for the working dogs,
especially like you,
to serve the world to some degree,
to have something to do.

There is a place not far from here
that's not yet widely known;
we ought to visit and you'll see
you're really not alone."

So thus, they made plans for a trip
and soundly slept that night.
Next morning they were full of beans
on rising at first light!

They ate a healthy breakfast then
prepared to venture towards
the place that Raven talked about
beyond the lakes and fjords.

"What fun we'll have," said Raven
as he glided through the pines,
"I haven't flapped my wings like this
since 1989!"

They made no haste, they took their time
with ample jubilation,
the journey being as vital as
the final destination.

They took the long and scenic route
through Mother Nature's land,
anticipating merrily
their purpose close at hand.

The trails and tracks of every sort
were filled with blooms and trees.
Enchanted scents infused the air
and travelled on the breeze.

The vistas were spectacular,
the sun was full and strong;
contented insects buzzed about
with merry birds in song.

With Icicle delighted to
thus journey with a friend,
indeed our hero's broken heart
would soon begin to mend.

30

Their forest trail came to an end
at Husky Haven's gate.
A lovely dog approached and spoke
to Raven and his mate:

"Hello! My name is Tikaboo!
I'll be your guide today.
You're very welcome to this ranch.
Now let's head off and play!

This place is made for hounds like us,
misunderstood, you see;
so go ahead, discover what
a dog like you can be."

So Icicle explored the ranch
and took in all the scenes
of other dogs pursuing the
adventures of his dreams.

And on those trails were fluffy dogs
just like our hero's sort
participating actively
in every kind of sport.

Some dogs were pulling folks on skis
on trails around the pond,
while others pulled a bike and towed
a boy or girl along.

Oh, how these dogs were having fun
on tracks of snow and grass!
Yet even more alluring was
up on the mountain pass!

34

For when our Husky saw the sleds,
the mushing in the snow,
he knew it was the thing for him
- he must give *that* a go!

And while those dogs were pulling sleds,
they howled in their delight!
Soon Icicle was mesmerised
by this uplifting sight!

They ran in twos and side by side -
a team in harmony.

When asked to take a left or right,
each Husky would agree.

These dogs were in their element
out running in the snow:
a job to do yet merriment,
at three degrees below!

36

With Icicle so occupied
so thrilled and having fun,
Wise Raven saw the time was right
to visit Foster Mum.

He came across Mum's little house
and found her in the yard.
He told himself he wouldn't nag -
he'd try so very hard!

He landed on a fence post and
politely gave his name,
explaining who he was and from
where recently he came.

He told Mum frankly why it was
her doggie fled from home,
then Husky Haven showed him that
he wasn't quite alone.

While Raven tried his hardest to
communicate and speak,
the only thing that she could hear
were raspy caws and squeaks!

40

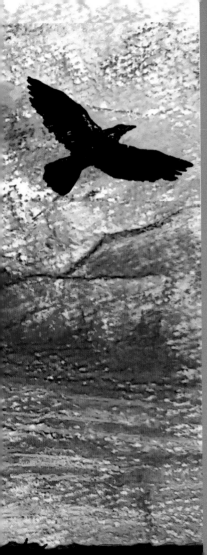

Her other clever foster dog
knew they should follow Raven
so they could find their Husky pal
let loose at Husky Haven.

He barked and pulled at Foster Mum
to get her rusty bike
so both of them could quickly
follow Raven on the hike.

And what a view awaited them!
A wealth of reds and blues,
the lakeshores glistening in the sun,
the hills with summer hues!

All three of them could feel the joy
of simply being outdoors -
no wonder little Icicle
would bolt right out the door!

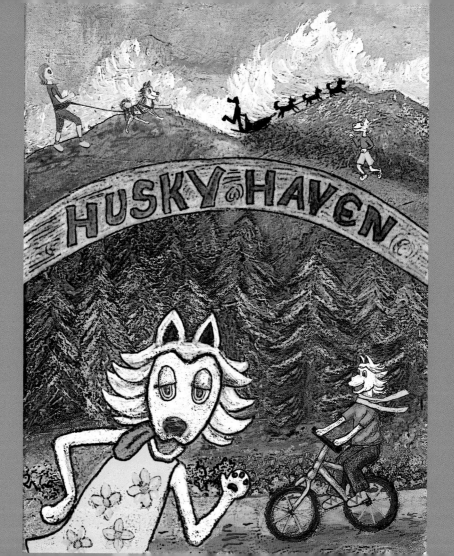

At last they reached the Husky ranch -
Miss Tikaboo was there:
the trails were packed with active dogs
and Huskies everywhere.

What sights for Foster Mum to see -
she clearly was agog!
Especially when she came across
another biking dog!

Ecstatic were these running hounds,
their little hearts fulfilled;
and then Mum saw her Icicle
out mushing up a hill!

In wonder, Mum saw for herself
how Icicle could run!
How swiftly he could pull that sled
while having lots of fun!

Her heart was full of pride for him
and everything made sense:
no wonder this athletic dog
would often hop the fence!

Despite the many times that he
had got lost in the past,
this time beloved Icicle
had found his way at last!

Then Icicle soon greeted them -
he'd missed his Mummy dear.
Not really sure how she'd react,
he tentatively came near:

She said :
"The last time that I saw you,
You were running through a farm!"
Then Foster Mum got off her bike ....

... and took him in her arms.

She said:

"I'm not surprised you came here
where you're free to run around,
while being inspired by many means
to be a happy hound!

You're clearly born to pull a sled
through miles and miles of snow!
You're meant for great adventures
and to run and move and GO!!

I know now you're a working dog,
a fact I can't ignore;
I can no longer treat you like
a sleepy Labrador!"

48

How Raven was so glad to see
this family unified,
with Icicle wrapped up in love,
his problems rectified.

50

This kind and understanding bird
could see his work was done.
He opened wide his jet black wings
and took off towards the sun.

Remember, if you feel confused,
directionless or low,
we all need help from time to time,
a friendly hand to hold.

We must all take the time to know
exactly who we are,
to look into our hearts and find
our own true shining star!

The End

Acknowledgements

Thank you to my family, especially my parents Phyllis & Edward and sister Ann, and to my friends for your loving support and belief that these tales had a place in the world!

The financial support raised through FundIt.ie allowed the printing and self-publishing of Tikaboo Tales to become a reality. I am so grateful for the kindness of all the funders.

A special "thank you" goes out to the
following generous funders:

Aleia & Robert
Joerg Assmann
Thomas & Susan Lamb Bean
Ann & Thobias Bergmann-Lynch
Marcela Bertrand
Gerard Cagney
Emily Doyle
Kristi K. Hagen
Barry Hingston
Laureann & Daniel Kelly
Paul Kuefler
The Montfort & Waltz Families
Valerie Murphy
Marian O'Brien for Project X Partners
Vivi Rogers
Sonja Straub